I Wear My Tutu Everywhere!

Grosset & Dunlap

For Beth with love—W.C.L.

For my father—M.M.

Published by Grosset & Dunlap, a division of Penguin Young Readers Group, 345 Hudson Street, New York, NY 10014.
GROSSET & DUNLAP is a trademark of Penguin Group (USA) Inc. Published simultaneously in Canada.
Printed in the U.S.A.

Library of Congress Cataloging-in-Publication Data
Lewison, Wendy Cheyette.
   I wear my tutu everywhere! / by Wendy Cheyette Lewison; illustrated by Mary Morgan.
     p. cm.
   Summary: When Tilly wants to wear her tutu all the time and rips it on the playground, Mama surprises her with the best
place to wear it—dancing class.
   [1. Ballet dancing—Fiction.] I. Morgan, Marv. 1957- ill. II. Title. III. Series.
   PZ7.L5884Iaad   1995
   [E]—dc20
                                                       94-36629
                                                       CIP
ISBN 0-448-40877-5   22 23 24 25 26 27 28 29 30   AC

I Wear My Tutu Everywhere!

By Wendy Cheyette Lewison

Illustrated by Mary Morgan

Grosset & Dunlap, Publishers

Once there was a little girl named Tilly who loved to dance.

She danced while Mama was braiding her hair.
"Please hold still," said Mama.

She danced while she was brushing her teeth.

And she danced in her dreams.

So, when Tilly's birthday came around, Mama
and Papa knew just what to give her for a present.

A tutu, a beautiful pink tutu to dance in—
just like a real ballerina!
It fit perfectly.

Tilly loved her new tutu. She loved it so much that she wore it wherever she went!

> *I love my tutu,*
> *I don't care,*
> *I wear my tutu*
> *everywhere!"*

sang Tilly, as she danced down the aisles at the supermarket.

In the frozen-food section it was pretty chilly. But Tilly didn't mind.

JUICE
$1.00

ICE CREAM BARS $1.99

ICE CREAM $3.00

CHOCOLATE ICE CREAM $1.50

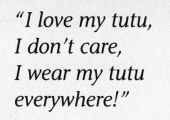

"I love my tutu,
I don't care,
I wear my tutu
everywhere!"

sang Tilly, as she bounced along on a hayride
with her family.
　"You look silly, Tilly," said her brother, Billy.
But Tilly didn't mind.

"I love my tutu,
I don't care,
I wear my tutu
everywhere!"

sang Tilly at the zoo. Then she
relevé-ed for the elephants . . .

. . . jeté-ed for the giraffes . . .

. . . and plié-ed for the penguins.

She wore her tutu to school.

She wore her tutu at the pool.

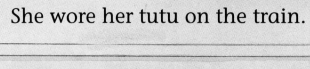

She wore her tutu on the train.

She wore her tutu in the rain.

She even wore her tutu
at the playground.
"It's too frilly, Tilly," said
her best friend, Milly.
But Tilly didn't mind.
Until . . . RRR-R-I-P!
Uh-oh! Tilly DID mind that!

So Mama had to fix Tilly's tutu.

And while she fixed it, Tilly had to wear her shorts to Milly's house. Her shorts were not as fancy as her tutu. But it *was* easier to ride her trike.

She had to wear her party dress to Willy's
birthday party. Everybody told her how pretty
she looked.

And she had to wear her pajamas to bed. Her pajamas were nice and soft to sleep in—not itchy and scratchy like her tutu.

By morning, Mama had Tilly's tutu all fixed. It looked brand-new! But that wasn't the only surprise Mama had for Tilly.

"I know just the perfect place for you to wear your tutu," said Mama. "It isn't the supermarket. It isn't the zoo. It isn't the school and it isn't the pool."

It was dancing class!
And that's where Tilly went in her tutu every
week, so she could learn how to dance . . .

. . . just like a real ballerina.